DINOSAUR RESCUE!

Triceratops

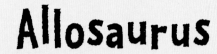

Allosaurus

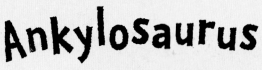

Iguanodon

Ankylosaurus

Carnotaurus

Megalosaurus

Stegosaurus

Baryonyx

Styracosaurus

Tyrannosaurus
rex

For Rick and Gill

First published 2014 by Nosy Crow Ltd
The Crow's Nest, 10a Lant Street
London SE1 1QR
www.nosycrow.com

ISBN 978 0 85763 166 4 (HB)
ISBN 978 0 85763 167 1 (PB)

A CIP catalogue record for this book is available from the British Library.

Printed in China

1 3 5 7 9 8 6 4 2

DINOSAUR RESCUE!

Penny Dale

nosy crow

Dinosaur train chugging,
chugging along the track.
Along the track, puffing out smoke.

Rescue dinosaurs rushing,
rushing to get there in time.
To get there in time,
before it's too late!

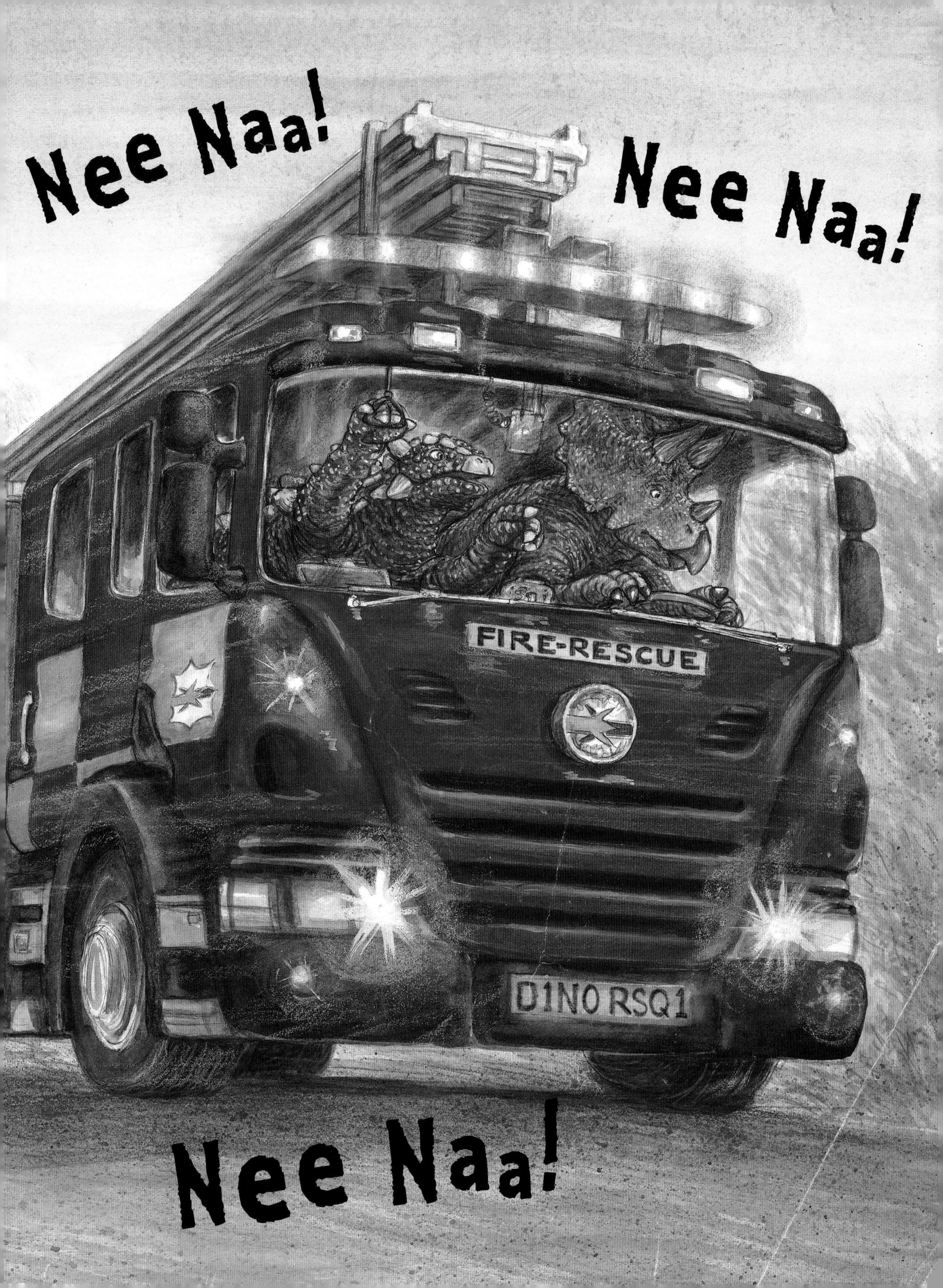
Nee Naa!
Nee Naa!
FIRE-RESCUE
D1NO RSQ1
Nee Naa!

Police dinosaurs racing,
racing to **stop** the train.
The **train** that is
heading for **trouble!**

Flying dinosaurs hovering,
hovering and swooping down.
Swooping down, ready to land!

Worried dinosaurs waving,
waving by the track.
By the track,
to stop the train!

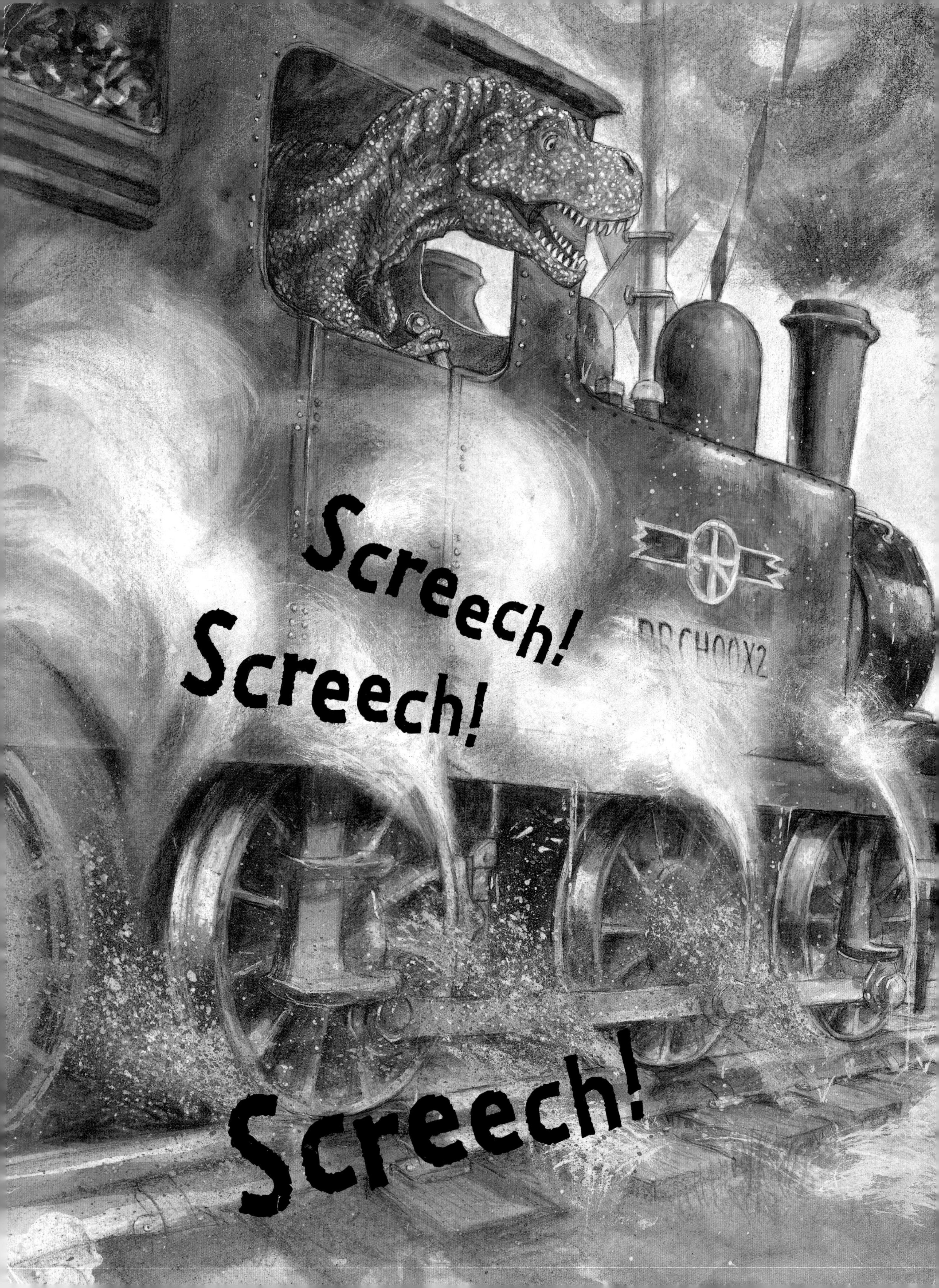
Screech!
Screech!
Screech!

Driver dinosaur braking,
braking very hard.
Very hard and stopping,
just…in…time!

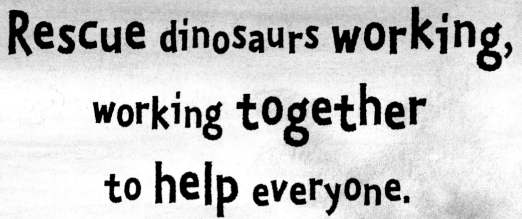

Rescue dinosaurs working,
working together
to help everyone.

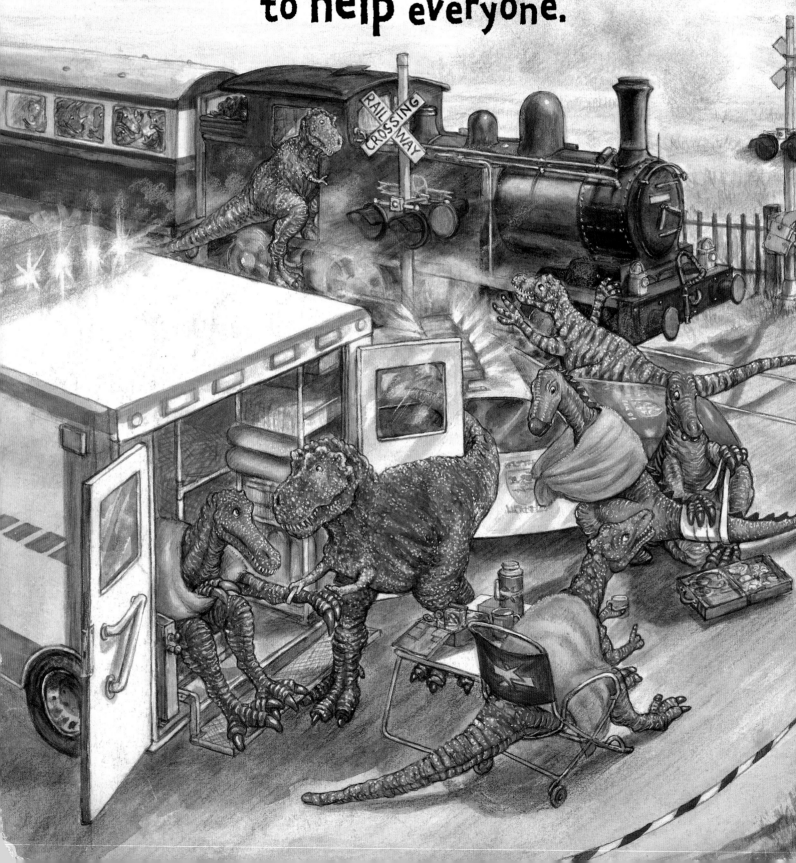

Breakdown dinosaurs lifting,
lifting and loading the truck.

Loading the truck and
towing it safely away.

Tired dinosaurs getting **back**,
back to **base**, at the **end** of the day.
Well done, Rescue Dinosaurs!

Hurray! Hurray!

Hurray!

Time to rest...

. . . time to play . . .

Fire
Engine

Pick-up Truck

Police
Car

Recovery
Truck

Ambulance

Steam
Engine

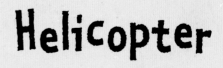

Helicopter